Oscar Wilde's

The
Happy Prince

Music by
DAVID PERKINS

Adaptation, Book & Lyrics by
CAROLINE DOOLEY
& DAVID PERKINS

SAMUEL FRENCH

FOUNDED 1830

NEW YORK HOLLYWOOD LONDON TORONTO

SAMUELFRENCH.COM

ISBN 978-0-573-66237-9   Printed in U.S.A.   #10183

**IMPORTANT BILLING AND CREDIT
REQUIREMENTS**

All producers of *THE HAPPY PRINCE must* give credit to the Author of the Play in all programs distributed in connection with performances of the Play, and in all instances in which the title of the Play appears for the purposes of advertising, publicizing or otherwise exploiting the Play and/or a production. The name of the Author *must* appear on a separate line on which no other name appears, immediately following the title and *must* appear in size of type not less than fifty percent of the size of the title type.

IMPORTANT INFORMATION

Alterations to the script and score

If changes, additions or cuts to the show are required to make it work for a particular group, any proposed alterations (no matter how small) MUST be approved by the authors before rehearsals commence. Approval can be sought via Samuel French Inc or directly from the authors via email: dperkins@dp-music.co.uk

The authors are happy to provide suggestions for such things as cuts, scene change music, chorus character names and so on. Making contact with them is easy and they will consider any request. Making small changes this way is free of charge and it turns an illegal alteration into a legal one.

Video and audio recordings

In certain circumstances, permission may be given for a video or audio recording of your show to be made. Please apply to Samuel French Inc for full details. Video and audio recordings made without prior permission are STRICTLY not allowed, even for archival or training purposes.

THE HAPPY PRINCE was first performed at the Yvonne Arnaud Theatre, Guildford, UK on 4th December 2003 by the Yvonne Arnaud Youth Theatre ACT 2 with the following cast:

HAPPY PRINCE	Nick Arnold
GOD	Mark Stewart
ANGEL	Ben Wattley
SEAMSTRESS	Therese Robinson
HER SON	Jack Sunderland
WRITER (MR WILDE)	Tim Slater
MATCH GIRL	Sarah Bowling
HER FATHER (MR SWANN)	Jacob Pierson
TEACHER (MISS PRISM)	Jo O'Malley
MAYOR	Ollie Dawe
TOWN CLERK	William Peters
COUNCILLORS	Guy Westbrook
	Jacob Pierson
THOMAS	Jeremy McCabe
CECILY	Natasha Grunert
SWALLOW	Jack Chard
TOWNSPEOPLE	Suzanna Britton (Charlotte)
	Yasmin Goodwin (Rose)
	Rebeccah Prince (Rosetta)
	Amy Stone (Amelia)
	Emily Zaborski (Mabel)
	Natasha Ho (Eliza)
	Sarah Churchlow (Sophia)
	Ruth Browton (Constance)
	Jenny Freyne (Eloise)
	Lauren Innes-Hill (Florence)
	Louise MacNamara (Lucretia)
	Karis Shepherd (Isobella)
	Sophie Cannings (Nancy)
	Emily Wenman (Adelaide)
	Jane Avis (Alice)
	Georgina Hellier (Gwendoline)
SCHOOL CHILDREN	Rebecca Wattley (Faith – Dreamy Child)
	Michael Cotton (Earnest)
	Ally Manson (Algernon)
	Frankie-May Webster (Hope)
	Jessica McCabe (Charity)

Directed by Julia Black
Musical Direction by David Perkins
Lighting & Sound Design by Justin Sutton

CHARACTERS

HAPPY PRINCE
GOD
ANGEL
SEAMSTRESS
SON
WRITER
MATCH GIRL
TEACHER
DREAMY CHILD
MAYOR
TOWN CLERK
THOMAS
CECILY
SWALLOW
EARNEST
MR SWANN

TOWNSPEOPLE
SCHOOL CHILDREN
COUNCILLORS

SCENES

Prologue: HEAVEN

Scene 1   IN THE TOWN SQUARE
(The Town Square)

Scene 2   WILL YOU HELP ME? (1) THE SEAMSTRESS
(The Town Square & the Seamstress's House)

Scene 3   THE RUBY IS DELIVERED
(The Town Square & the Seamstress's House)

Scene 4   ORNITHOLOGY LESSON
(The Town Square)

Scene 5   WILL YOU HELP ME? (2) THE WRITER
(The Town Square & the Writer's Attic)

Scene 6   ANGEL/MAYOR/TOWNSPEOPLE CROSSOVER
(The Town Square)

Scene 7   WILL YOU HELP ME? (3) THE MATCH GIRL
(The Town Square continued)

Scene 8   WILL YOU HELP ME? (4) GOLD LEAF FROM HEAVEN
(The Town Square)

Scene 9   THE MAYOR'S BALL
(The Ballroom at the Town Hall)

Epilogue: HEAVEN

NOTE: An interval can be inserted between Scenes 5 & 6

MUSICAL NUMBERS

OVERTURE

1   WAITING FOR THE MAYOR
(Townspeople, School Children, Town Clerk)

2   MAYOR'S SONG
(Mayor, Town Clerk, Thomas, Cecily, Councillors, Townspeople, School Children)

2a   EXIT OF MAYOR/UNDERSCORE /
(Reprise #1) HIGH ABOVE STANDS A STATUE *(Dreamy Child)* / UNDERSCORE

3   I'VE A LONG WAY TO GO *(Swallow)*

4   LULLABY OF DREAMS *(Seamstress)*

4a   SCENE CHANGE MUSIC

5   HOW WONDERFUL THE STARS ARE
(Thomas, Cecily, Happy Prince, Townspeople, Seamstress, Son)

6   BIRD SONG *(Teacher, School Children)*

6a   EXIT

6b   UNDERSCORE

7   WHERE'S THE PLAY? / HOW CAN I WRITE?
(Town Clerk / Writer)

7a   FLY LITTLE SWALLOW *(Happy Prince)* / UNDERSCORE

7b   UNDERSCORE /
(Reprise #2) HIGH ABOVE STANDS A STATUE *(Dreamy Child)*

8   MATCHES FOR SALE *(Match Girl)*

8a   (Reprise) MATCHES FOR SALE *(Match Girl, Happy Prince)*

9   GOLDEN LEAVES *(Townspeople, School Children, Happy Prince)*

9a   (Reprise) I'VE A LONG WAY TO GO *(Swallow)*

9b   SCENE CHANGE MUSIC

9c   DANCE MUSIC (UNDERSCORE)

10   WHEN YOUR DREAM IS IN SIGHT *(Seamstress, Son, Writer, Teacher, Match Girl, Mr Swann, Townspeople, School Children, Councillors)*

10a   BOWS

10b   (Encore) WHEN YOUR DREAM IS IN SIGHT *(Company)*

10c   EXIT

SYNOPSIS

The show opens with **God** practising his golf swings in Heaven. A new **Angel** arrives and God explains that in order to receive his wings - the ultimate accolade for every novice angel - he must perform a challenge. The angel is to return to earth and bring back the two most precious things he can find.

Meanwhile the **Townspeople** are meeting in the old Town Square to await the arrival of their newly elected Mayor (**Waiting for the Mayor**). They hope he will be good to them and bring them much needed prosperity. Overlooking the square is a beautiful statue of the **Happy Prince**. The Townspeople idolise him as he seems to be the only person in the world who is truly happy.

The **Mayor** arrives with the **Town Clerk** and the **Town Councillors** to give his inaugural speech (**Mayor's Song**). He also states that his daughter Cecily is to marry **Thomas Cardew** the richest man in the city and invites them to a celebratory Ball, for which tickets cost two guineas. The Townspeople are not impressed. They wish they could be as happy as the Happy Prince. The **Dreamy Child** sings in admiration of the beautiful statue (**High Above Stands a Statue**) and claims that he 'looks like an angel'.

A **Swallow** arrives on the scene. He is on his way to Egypt to escape the winter weather and is looking for a place to spend the night (**I've a Long Way to Go**). He tries to sleep at the feet of the Happy Prince but is woken by teardrops falling from the statue's eyes. The Happy Prince explains he is sad because being up so high he can see all the misery of the city. He can see a **Seamstress** struggling to finish a Ball gown for Cecily, but she is poor and has a very ill **Son**. She is singing him a lullaby (**Lullaby of Dreams**).

The Happy Prince asks the Swallow to take the ruby from his sword-hilt and give it to the Seamstress. The Swallow reluctantly agrees, removes the ruby and flies off.

Down in the square Cecily and Thomas are out for an evening stroll. Thomas, who is more interested in star-gazing and bird-watching than romance, notices the Swallow but mistakes the ruby for a red beak. He is amazed and sings in admiration. He is also transfixed by the night sky (**How Wonderful the Stars Are**). The Townspeople enter and are equally astounded by the unusual bird and the beautiful stars.

The Seamstress discovers the ruby in her embroidery and looks out of the window to see who might have brought it to her. Her Son feels a little better – he dreamt that a bird was fanning his head with its wings. The Swallow returns to the statue and despite the cold weather feels warmed by the good deed he has done.

The following day we see the Mayor and his Councillors. They are warning him that the Townspeople are getting restless because conditions in the town are not improving. The **Teacher** enters with her **School**

Children. They are trying to find the unusual bird that she saw the night before. The children spot it and identify it as being a swallow. The Teacher says it cannot possibly be a swallow because it would have left these shores for a warmer climate by now. She sings a song listing all the possible birds it could be **(Bird Song)** whilst the children continue to insist that it is a swallow. Eventually she comes to her own conclusion that it is in fact a swallow.

In the evening the Happy Prince asks the Swallow to help him again by taking a sapphire – one of his eyes – to a penniless **Writer** who is trying to finish a play in time for the children to perform at the Mayor's Ball. We see the Writer trying to work, but he is too cold and hungry. The Town Clerk pays a visit and is annoyed that the play is not finished **(Where's the Play?/How Can I Write?)**. The Writer is desperate. The Swallow agrees to help – he plucks out the sapphire and flies away to the Writer **(Fly Little Swallow)**. The Writer discovers the sapphire in the dying embers of the grate and is confident that he will be able to finish his play as he can now afford food and firewood.

The Dreamy Child appears in the square to gaze again at the Happy Prince and sees the Angel who has been observing things. She is delighted.

The Angel is annoyed that he has been spotted and is frustrated that he cannot find anything precious. He phones Heaven (on his mobile phone) to ask for help but cannot get hold of God – he has taken the day off to play golf!

Back in the square the Mayor is annoyed that no one has bought any tickets for the Ball – the Town Clerk explains that the Townspeople are not able to afford the two guineas. The Dreamy Child tells a group of children that she has seen an angel. They tease her about it and a chase ensues. A little **Match Girl** enters trying to sell her wares. She sings a little song and we hear about her tough, lonely life **(Matches For Sale)**. The children run past her knocking her matches into the gutter – they are ruined and she knows that her father will beat her when she gets home.

The Happy Prince once more asks the Swallow for help. The Swallow is concerned about the weather but agrees to help by taking the Prince's other eye to the Match Girl. Down in the square the Match Girl discovers the sapphire in one of her match boxes. She is saved.

The Swallow tells the Happy Prince that it is now too late for him to leave – the snows of winter will be here soon and he will never make it to Egypt now. The statue asks for help one last time – he is decorated with fine gold and instructs the Swallow to remove it leaf by leaf and give it to the poor people of the city. This he does. The Townspeople are overjoyed and sing joyously in the square below as the golden leaves fall from the sky **(Golden Leaves)**.

The Swallow returns to the statue, now very cold and weak. He sings a last song **(Reprise: I've a Long Way to Go)** and drops down dead at the feet of the statue. The Happy Prince's heart breaks.

It is the night of the Ball. The Mayor asks his Councillors what the commotion was about last night. They inform him that some sort of miracle had taken place. He is disgruntled and equally dismayed by the drabness of the Happy Prince. The last straw is the sight of a dead bird at the Statue's feet. He instructs a councillor to remove the dead bird, melt down the statue and use the metal to build a statue of him.

At the Ball, we see the School Children performing the closing moments of the Writer's new play – The Selfish Giant. The Mayor approves but suggests it might work better as a short story. He is introduced to the Seamstress, her Son, the Match Girl and her father, **Mr Swann.** The Mayor is both curious and envious to hear about their good fortunes – equally he cannot understand how all the Townspeople suddenly could afford the two guineas and come to the Ball. He is thankful that his daughter is about to marry a very rich man. Meanwhile, Cecily is annoyed at Thomas because he still keeps talking about astronomy. She gives him an ultimatum – is he going to gaze at the stars or at her?

The dancing commences. A councillor enters and informs the Mayor that when melting down the statue of the Happy Prince, the foundry was left with a broken lead heart. The Mayor instructs him to throw it on the rubbish heap along with the dead bird. At that moment Cecily slaps Thomas and announces that 'the wedding is off'. The Mayor is ruined and leaves in despair. The dancing re-commences and the guests sing a celebratory song (**When Your Dream is in Sight**).

Back in Heaven, the Angel returns with a box containing the two most precious things that he could find – the dead Swallow and the broken lead heart from the statue of the Happy Prince. God reassures the Angel that he has chosen well for 'in my garden of paradise this little bird will always sing and in my city of gold the Prince will be truly happy again'. The Angel will be rewarded by getting his wings.

God takes the heart of the Prince and places it in his pocket. He then takes the Swallow and gently releases him into his garden. We hear the sound of bird song fill the air, rising to a crescendo and then fading into nothing.

DIRECTOR'S NOTES

CHARACTER BREAKDOWN
(including costume suggestions & scene / song involvement)

HAPPY PRINCE
A 'living' golden statue played by a young actor. His outwardly happy appearance hides an inner sadness. He is required to maintain a frozen position for long periods of time, therefore physical strength and control is required.
COSTUME SUGGESTIONS: Golden clothes fit for a prince; sword attached to belt
SCENES: All scenes except Prologue, Scene 9, Epilogue
SONGS: How Wonderful the Stars Are (solo), Fly Little Swallow (solo), (Reprise) Matches for Sale (solo), Golden Leaves (solo), (Encore) When Your Dream is in Sight

GOD
The main man! He rules Heaven and Earth with military precision. He is firm but fair and a very keen golfer.
COSTUME SUGGESTIONS: Natty double-breasted white suit and tie, white shoes
SCENES: Prologue, Epilogue
SONGS: (Encore) When Your Dream is in Sight

ANGEL
A recently recruited angel, anxious to achieve his honorary wings from God. He is young and naïve and is daunted by the challenge God sets him.
COSTUME SUGGESTIONS: White boiler suit or white sweatshirt with dungarees
SCENES: Prologue, 1, 3, 5, 6, 7, 8, Epilogue
SONGS: (Encore) When Your Dream is in Sight

SEAMSTRESS
A loving and caring mother who works very hard to support her ill son. Despite her poverty she maintains a hopeful outlook.
COSTUME SUGGESTIONS: Long dress, apron, shawl
SCENES: 1, 2, 3, 8, 9
SONGS: Waiting for the Mayor, Mayor's Song, Lullaby of Dreams (solo), How Wonderful the Stars Are, Golden Leaves, When Your Dream is in Sight (duet), (Encore) When Your Dream is in Sight

SON
The Seamstress's poorly child. He engenders sympathy from the audience.
COSTUME SUGGESTIONS: Trousers, shirt (scene 2), plus jacket for other scenes
SCENES: 1, 2, 3, 8, 9
SONGS: Waiting for the Mayor, Mayor's Song, How Wonderful the Stars

Are, Golden Leaves, When Your Dream is in Sight (duet), (Encore) When Your Dream is in Sight

WRITER

An aspiring playwright. He is battling with cold and hunger in his struggle to finish his play. He has almost given up hope.

COSTUME SUGGESTIONS: Scruffy suit, scarf and fingerless gloves

SCENES: 1, 3, 5, 8, 9

SONGS: Waiting for the Mayor, Mayor's Song, How Wonderful the Stars Are, Where's the Play? / How Can I Write? (solo), Golden Leaves, When Your Dream is in Sight (duet), (Encore) When Your Dream is in Sight

MATCH GIRL

A young, hard-working street seller. She leads a tough and lonely life with no friends and is in fear of her father.

COSTUME SUGGESTIONS: Shabby dress, bare-footed

SCENES: 1, 3, 6, 7, 8, 9

SONGS: Waiting for the Mayor, Mayor's Song, How Wonderful the Stars Are, Matches for Sale (solo), (Reprise) Matches for Sale (solo), Golden Leaves, When Your Dream is in Sight (duet), (Encore) When Your Dream is in Sight

TEACHER

A strict and slightly eccentric lady who is very committed to her profession. She is well spoken and has a confident, sometimes arrogant manner.

COSTUME SUGGESTIONS: A well-tailored suit (long skirt), gloves, hat and pince-nez / spectacles

SCENES: 1, 4, 8, 9

SONGS: Waiting for the Mayor, Mayor's Song, How Wonderful the Stars Are, Bird Song (solo), Golden Leaves, When Your Dream is in Sight (duet), (Encore) When Your Dream is in Sight

DREAMY CHILD

A small girl with a big imagination. She endures much teasing from her peers but remains resolute in her beliefs.

COSTUME SUGGESTIONS: (See School Children below)

SCENES: 1, 4, 5, 6, 8, 9

SONGS: Waiting for the Mayor, Mayor's Song, (Reprise #1) High Above Stands a Statue (solo), Bird Song, (Reprise #2) High Above Stands a Statue (solo), Golden Leaves, When Your Dream is in Sight, (Encore) When Your Dream is in Sight

MAYOR

A bumptious, self-important autocrat with an insatiable greed for power and money. He treats everyone with disdain.

COSTUME SUGGESTIONS: Mayoral robes, edged with ermine. Ruffle-fronted shirt, double-pointed hat and chain

SCENES: 1, 4, 6, 8, 9

SONGS: Mayor's Song (solo), (Encore) When Your Dream is in Sight

TOWN CLERK

An ambitious, grovelling man. He is desperate for recognition from the Mayor and will do all he can to achieve this. He has an overinflated sense of self-importance.

COSTUME SUGGESTIONS: Black tail-coated suit, waistcoat, cravat and top hat

SCENES: 1, 4, 5, 7, 8, 9

SONGS: Waiting for the Mayor, Mayor's Song, Where's the Play? / How Can I Write? (solo), (Encore) When Your Dream is in Sight

THOMAS

A wealthy and studious young man, more passionate about astronomy and ornithology than about his fiancée, Cecily.

COSTUME SUGGESTIONS: Smart tail-coat, trousers, shirt, cravat and top hat

SCENES: 1, 3, 9

SONGS: Mayor's Song, How Wonderful the Stars Are (solo), (Encore) When Your Dream is in Sight

CECILY

The Mayor's spoilt daughter. She is self-centred and demands attention from everyone, especially Thomas.

COSTUME SUGGESTIONS: Beautifully made dress (or jacket and long skirt), hat, gloves

SCENES: 1, 3, 9

SONGS: Mayor's Song, (Encore) When Your Dream is in Sight

SWALLOW

A lively, talkative, 'cheeky chappy' bird played by a small boy or girl. Although he is single-minded and determined, he succumbs to the Happy Prince's demands because of his soft heart and kindly nature.

COSTUME SUGGESTIONS: Shabby tail-coat with feathered sleeves, red cravat, ragged trousers, bare feet and black hat

SCENES: 2, 3, 4, 5, 7, 8

SONGS: I've a Long Way to Go (solo), (Reprise) I've a Long Way to Go (solo)

EARNEST

An extremely clever young child. He has a unsettling maturity born out of his superior intellect.

COSTUME SUGGESTIONS: Spectacles. (See School Children below)

SCENES: 1, 4, 8, 9

SONGS: Waiting for the Mayor, Mayor's Song, Bird Song, Golden Leaves, When Your Dream is in Sight, (Encore) When Your Dream is in Sight

MR SWANN

The Match Girl's father. He is a tough man who has worked hard all his life and expects his daughter to do the same.

COSTUME SUGGESTIONS: (See Townspeople below)

SCENES: 1, 3, 8, 9

SONGS: When Your Dream is in Sight (duet), (Encore) When Your Dream is in Sight

TOWNSPEOPLE

The many and various people that live and work in the town – any number, all ages. Roles can include shopkeepers, street sellers, road sweepers, policemen, residents etc. Family groups can be formed using actors of differing ages. In the script, the Seamstress, her Son, the Teacher, the Writer, Mr Swann and the Match Girl are regarded as Townspeople except where specified.

COSTUME SUGGESTIONS: Appropriate clothes to denote their role in the town, but with a general sombre look and an air of poverty. For the Ball scene (scene 9), they can add masks and something to display their newly-found wealth

SCENES: 1, 3, 6, 8, 9

SONGS: Waiting for the Mayor, Mayor's Song, How Wonderful the Stars Are, Golden Leaves, When Your Dream is in Sight, (Encore) When Your Dream is in Sight

SCHOOL CHILDREN

A group of smartly uniformed children. They are well disciplined by the Teacher but their individual personalities shine through.

COSTUME SUGGESTIONS: Girls – black skirts, black long-sleeve tops, white pinafore, black tights, black shoes, hats if desired. Boys – black knee-length trousers, black waistcoat, white shirt, hats if desired. In the Ball scene (scene 9) the child playing the 'Giant' wears a long costume and a false beard. The child playing the 'Small Boy' wears a simple white tunic

SCENES: 1, 4, 8, 9

SONGS: Waiting for the Mayor, Mayor's Song, Bird Song, Golden Leaves, When Your Dream is in Sight, (Encore) When Your Dream is in Sight

COUNCILLORS

A small group of long-suffering civil servants. They are ruled by the Mayor and bullied by the Town Clerk because they try to represent the Townspeople in their needs.

COSTUME SUGGESTIONS: Black gowns, black trousers, white shirts, cravats, waistcoats and tricorn hats

SCENES: 1, 4, 6, 8, 9

SONGS: Mayor's Song, When Your Dream is in Sight, (Encore) When Your Dream is in Sight

SET / STAGING SUGGESTIONS

The Happy Prince can be performed with a minimum amount of stage settings. There are five locations where the action takes place, here are a few suggestions including ideas for scenery/furniture/dressing etc. See also Furniture & Property list page 76.

(a) Heaven.
A designated area is required to represent Heaven. This could be the entire downstage area separated from the rest of the stage by a gauze or star-cloth that is flown in or a smaller area to one side of the stage. For a good effect, this area could be raised up onto a higher level.

(b) The Town Square.
The main part of the stage or performing area. A plinth or platform is needed for the Happy Prince to stand on – upstage centre is the most effective place – with enough room in front and behind for action to take place. If resources allow, the Townspeople could have market stalls, barrows etc but they would need to be easily removable to allow slick scene changes. There could be a 'townscape' ground row at the very rear of the stage to represent the buildings and side flats with more buildings painted on to give a deeper perspective. The Town Hall could be represented by one of these. Cobbles could be painted on the stage to give a greater urban feel and stars could be flown into this area for great effect during scene 3. The original production used fibre optic lights to achieve this effect. A glitter drop set above the Town Square should be used if possible for the gold-leaf falling from Heaven in scene 8. If preferred this could be achieved with a lighting effect.

(c) The Seamstress's House.
A simple area downstage right or left with intimate lighting. A bed and a chair is all that is required to create this scene. The audience need to see and hear the Happy Prince during this scene, so the setting cannot be too elaborate or be directly in front of him.

(d) The Writer's Attic.
A simple area downstage right or left with subdued lighting. See Furniture & Property list page 76 for details. An unmasked view of the Happy Prince is essential for this setting.

(e) The Ballroom at the Town Hall.
The main part of the stage. A ballroom backcloth could be used and chandeliers flown in if money is no object, but it could also be done very simply with colourful dressing brought on by the company. To allow a quick scene change into the Ball scene, the plinth can remain on the stage and be used by the School Children when they perform their play.

LIGHTING

Great effects and atmosphere can be achieved through lighting and if used thoughtfully it can reduce the need for elaborate scenery. The ability to isolate individual areas of the stage with the creative use of 'specials', stage 'washes', follow-spots, glitter balls and 'gobos' will add a great deal to the performance and the audience's enjoyment.

FURNITURE & PROPERTIES

A list of furniture and properties can be found on page 76. Many are essential to the show and can be as simple or elaborate as resources allow. Others can be added at the discretion of the director.

EFFECTS

An effects plot can be found on page 77.

Most sound effects are created by the percussion player in the band and are indicated in the script and score. If preferred these effects could be made by members of the cast / stage crew or could be pre-recorded.

The show ends with the sound effect of birdsong rising to a crescendo then fading into nothing. This important sound effect is available from Samuel French Inc.

MUSIC NOTES

Metronome markings have been printed in the score to indicate the tempo for the music. In order to recreate the correct feel for each song it is essential that these are adhered to **as closely as possible.**

A demo CD of the songs can be hired from Samuel French Inc. This recording must be used for perusal and learning purposes only and not for playback during a performance.

INSTRUMENTATION

The piano/conductor score is available for hire from Samuel French Inc and should be used for rehearsal purposes and performance accompaniment.

The instrumentation for 8 players is as follows

Piano / Conductor
Reed I   (Flute db. Clarinet)
Reed II   (Flute db. Clarinet, Bass Clarinet)
Reed III   (Oboe db. Cor Anglais)
Trumpet   (db. Flugelhorn)
Violin
Double Bass
Drums/Percussion   (Drum kit, Glockenspiel, 2 Pedal Timpani, Triangle, Mark Tree, Wood Block, Duck Call)

The instrumentation can be reduced to Piano only, or Piano, Bass & Drums / Perc. No other combination will work

Band parts are available for hire from Samuel French Inc.

ACKNOWLEDGEMENTS

The authors would like to thank the following people:

Julia Black
Vivien Goodwin and Amanda Smith (Samuel French Ltd, London)
James Barber and the Yvonne Arnaud Theatre, Guildford
The YAT Youth Theatre kids (and their parents!)

and not forgetting…

Oscar Wilde himself!

Dedicated to
Connie, Ella, Scott and Hugo

.

The story is set in the timeless place known as Heaven and at various locations in a small city in the late 19th century. See set / staging suggestions, page 16. Furniture and properties are suggested in the script but there is a full list on page 76.

OVERTURE

Dry ice / smoke effects start

Prologue   HEAVEN

God is revealed, cheerily whistling an appropriate tune and gently practising his golf putting. The Angel enters

GOD. Do come in. You're the new arrival aren't you?

ANGEL. Yes, Sir. Number 4962. I got here this morning.

GOD. Good journey? Not too much turbulence I hope?

ANGEL. A little, but nothing too unsettling.

GOD. Good. Well, take a seat. Welcome to the place that the people down there call Heaven. Up here, we simply refer to it as home. After all, home is where the heart is, so they say.

ANGEL. So they say, Sir.

GOD. Now, all our trainee angels have to undergo a simple challenge in order to receive their wings.

ANGEL. Yes, Sir.

GOD. Oh, please, just call me God.

ANGEL. Yes, Sir. I mean God, Sir.

GOD. Now, you need to understand the importance of this challenge. Wings are vital to an angel – without them you're just like any other immortal. With them you can really go places!

ANGEL. Yes …God. I understand. But what exactly do I have to do?

GOD. This is your challenge. You are to return to earth and bring back the two most precious things that you can find.

ANGEL. But God, I've only just got here.

GOD. I know. You thought life was tough, but death is much more challenging.

ANGEL. And there I was, looking forward to putting my feet up with a nice cup of tea and an angel cake.

GOD. Don't worry 4962, once you've completed your task you'll have plenty of time to settle in properly … (*Laughing*) an Eternity in fact.

ANGEL. But what exactly am I meant to bring back?

GOD. Well, that's for you to decide. But choose wisely. You must find the two things that in your opinion are the most precious and bring them back to me. You have three days to complete this task.

ANGEL. Three days? That's not very long.

GOD. Not very long? I created the whole lot in seven – and that included a day off!

ANGEL. Yes, I know. But you're … Well, you're … (*He is struggling to find the appropriate word*)

GOD. God. That's right. Now off you go, chop, chop.

The Angel exits. The dry ice / smoke effects stop

God taps an imaginary hotel reception bell. There is a percussion effect, eg triangle

GOD. Next!

Scene 1   **IN THE TOWN SQUARE**
                   (The Town Square)

SONG 1   *WAITING FOR THE MAYOR*

During the musical introduction the Townspeople (including the School Children) enter the town square and begin to gather around the statue of the Happy Prince. They are waiting for the arrival of the newly elected Mayor

TOWNSPEOPLE.

> COME ALONG, HURRY TO THE OLD TOWN SQUARE
> DON'T DELAY, QUICKLY, DON'T BE LATE
> WE'VE GOT TO RUSH, GOT TO SEE OUR BRAND NEW MAYOR
> GIVE HIS SPEECH, THEN WE'LL KNOW OUR FATE
> HERE TODAY, HE WILL SAY JUST WHAT HE THINKS
> WE'LL FIND OUT WHAT HE PLANS TO DO
> HE'S MADE IT QUITE CLEAR, HE'S HERE FOR A YEAR
> GET READY TO CHEER OR BOO!

TOWNSPERSON.

> WILL HE LISTEN AND TRY TO DO HIS BEST?

TOWNSPERSON.

> SOLVE OUR PROBLEMS OR BE JUST LIKE THE REST?

TOWNSPEOPLE.

> WHAT WE'RE HOPING FOR IS A KIND AND THOUGHTFUL MAN
> WHO WILL CARE FOR US AND DO EVERYTHING HE CAN

TOWNSPEOPLE (A).

> BUT IF HE IS MEAN AND SELFISH THEN WE WON'T KNOW WHAT TO DO

TOWNSPEOPLE (B).

> IF THE MAYOR IS MEAN AND SELFISH

(A) & (B).

THEN THERE'S NOTHING WE CAN DO

TOWNSPERSON.

HIGH ABOVE STANDS A STATUE OF A BOY

GOLDEN, BRIGHT, SMILING IN THE SUN

THE HAPPY PRINCE FILLS OUR DAYS WITH HOPE AND JOY

SHARING HIS LOVE WITH EVERYONE

TOWNSPEOPLE.

WILL THE MAYOR GUIDE US LIKE THE STATUE DOES?

CARE FOR US IN EVERYTHING WE DO?

HE'S HERE FOR A WHILE, LET'S HOPE HE CAN SMILE

GET READY TO CHEER OR BOO!

TOWNSPERSON.

WILL HE TAKE ALL THE MONEY THAT WE EARN?

TOWNSPERSON.

LEAVE US HUNGRY, WITHOUT THE LEAST CONCERN?

TOWNSPEOPLE.

WHAT WE'RE HOPING FOR IS A STRONG AND GUIDING LIGHT

LIKE THE HAPPY PRINCE, THROUGH THE DAY AND THROUGH THE NIGHT

TOWNSPEOPLE (A).

BUT IF HE IS MEAN AND SELFISH THEN WE WON'T KNOW WHAT TO DO

TOWNSPEOPLE (B).

BUT IF HE IS MEAN AND SELFISH THEN WE WON'T KNOW WHAT TO DO

TOWNSPEOPLE (A).

IF THE MAYOR IS MEAN AND SELFISH

(A) & (B).

THEN THERE'S NOTHING WE CAN DO

UNDERSCORE continues

SEAMSTRESS. I hope he can help the poor people in our town. The rich have so much and others so little.

WRITER. I hope he supports writers like me. I find it so difficult to make a decent living.

MATCH GIRL. I really need someone to help me – I work so hard for next to nothing.

TEACHER. I hope he gives some money to the school. The roof needs repairing and my pupils need new books.

TOWNSPERSON. We must have a new hospital built.

(The crowd murmur in agreement)

TOWNSPERSON. We need a park for the children to play in.

(The children agree enthusiastically)

TOWNSPERSON. We need someone like the Happy Prince who will really watch over us.

(The crowd cheer in agreement)

SONG continues

TOWNSPEOPLE.
WILL THE MAYOR GUIDE US LIKE THE STATUE DOES?
CARE FOR US IN EVERYTHING WE DO?
HE'S HERE FOR A WHILE, LET'S HOPE HE CAN SMILE
GET READY TO CHEER OR BOO!
HE'S MADE IT QUITE CLEAR, HE'S HERE FOR A YEAR
GET READY TO CHEER OR BOO!

The Town Clerk enters

TOWN CLERK.
(Spoken) STAND ASIDE FOR THE MAYOR IS HERE
ON THE COUNT OF THREE YOU CHEER

TOWNSPEOPLE (A).
(Sung) IT'S THE MAYOR!

TOWNSPEOPLE (B).
IT'S THE MAYOR!

TOWNSPEOPLE (A).
IS HE THERE?

TOWNSPEOPLE (B).
IS HE THERE?

TOWNSPEOPLE (A).	TOWNSPEOPLE (B).
GIVE A CHEER	IS HE COMING?
FOR THE	IS HE COMING?
MAYOR	IS HE COMING?
IS	IS HE COMING
HERE!	HERE?

(A) & (B).
THE MAYOR IS HERE!

TOWN CLERK. One, two, three

SONG 2   MAYOR'S SONG

The Town Clerk gestures to the crowd that they should cheer and they do. The Mayor, the Councillors, the Mayor's daughter Cecily and her fiancé Thomas enter.

Thomas studies his astronomy book throughout the scene

MAYOR.
I AM THRILLED AND QUITE DELIGHTED TO STAND
UP HERE TODAY
MY TERM AS MAYOR HAS STARTED, THERE ARE LOTS
OF THINGS TO SAY
BUT FIRST AND MOST IMPORTANT, IF YOU WANT TO
BEND MY EAR
YOU MUST ALWAYS SAY 'YOUR HONOUR' AND TRY
TO BE SINCERE
IT'S A VERY SIMPLE TASK, TO DO THE THINGS I ASK
YOU MUST ALWAYS SAY 'YOUR HONOUR', LET'S
MAKE THAT VERY CLEAR

I WON'T SUFFER FOOLS, YOU WILL STICK TO THE
RULES
YOU MUST ALWAYS CALL ME 'YOUR HONOUR'

TOWN CLERK/ COUNCILLORS/ THOMAS/CECILY.	TOWNSPEOPLE (A).	TOWNSPEOPLE (B).
HE WON'T SUFFER FOOLS, YOU WILL STICK TO THE RULES YOU MUST ALWAYS CALL HIM 'YOUR HONOUR'	HE WON'T SUFFER FOOLS, WE WILL STICK TO THE RULES WE MUST ALWAYS CALL HIM 'YOUR HONOUR'	HE WON'T SUFFER FOOLS, WE WILL STICK TO THE RULES WE MUST ALWAYS CALL HIM 'YOUR HONOUR'

MAYOR.

THEY'RE ALL UNAWARE
THAT WHILE I AM MAYOR
I WON'T DO A THING FOR THEM, I SIMPLY DO NOT
CARE

TOWNSPEOPLE.

WITH ALL DUE RESPECT
THIS HAS NO EFFECT
WE'RE QUITE UNIMPRESSED WITH OUR NEW MAYOR-
ELECT

MAYOR.

NOW I KNOW THE POOR ARE HUNGRY AND THERE'S
NOT ENOUGH TO EAT
AND THE TOWN IS VERY DIRTY WITH LITTER IN THE
STREET
BUT I HAVE TO SPEAK QUITE FRANKLY, THERE'S A
JOB YOU ALL CAN DO
YOU MUST WORK A LITTLE HARDER, UNTIL EACH
DAY IS THROUGH

IF YOU WANT FOR BETTER HEALTH AND A HIGHER

STATE OF WEALTH
YOU MUST WORK A LITTLE HARDER, I'LL LEAVE IT
UP TO YOU

THERE IS NO 'EITHER-OR', YOU WILL STICK TO THE
LAW
YOU MUST WORK A LITTLE HARDER

TOWN CLERK/ COUNCILLORS/ THOMAS/CECILY.	TOWNSPEOPLE (A).	TOWNSPEOPLE (B).
THERE IS NO 'EITHER-OR'		
YOU WILL STICK TO THE LAW	THERE IS NO 'EITHER-OR	
YOU MUST WORK A LITTLE HARDER	WE WILL STICK TO THE LAW	THERE IS NO 'EITHER-OR'
	WE MUST WORK A LITTLE HARDER	WE WILL STICK TO THE LAW
		WE MUST WORK A LITTLE HARDER

MAYOR.

NOW HERE IS MY PLAN
I'LL SEE IF I CAN
CONVINCE THEM WHAT A VERY, VERY CLEVER MAN I
AM

TOWNSPEOPLE.

WE OUGHT TO BEWARE
THE MAYOR DOESN'T CARE
HE THINKS WE ARE LAZY, IT SIMPLY ISN'T FAIR

MAYOR/TC/ COUNCILLORS/ THOMAS/CECILY.	TOWNSPEOPLE.
I/HE	
WON'T SUFFER	
FOOLS,	
YOU WILL	WE
STICK TO THE	WON'T SUFFER
RULES	FOOLS,
YOU MUST	AND WE
ALWAYS CALL	DON'T LIKE
ME/HIM 'YOUR	THE RULES 'YOUR
HONOUR'	HONOUR'
THERE IS NO	
'EITHER-	
OR'	
YOU WILL	THERE IS
STICK TO THE	NO 'EITHER-
LAW	OR'
YOU MUST	WE WON'T
DO AS YOU	DO AS WE
ARE TOLD!	ARE TOLD!

	TOWNSPEOPLE (A).	TOWNSPEOPLE (B).
I/HE		WE...
WON'T SUFFER		
FOOLS,		
YOU WILL	WE	
STICK TO THE	WON'T SUFFER	DON'T
RULES	FOOLS,	SUFFER
YOU MUST	AND WE	
ALWAYS CALL	DON'T LIKE	FOOLS
ME/HIM 'YOUR	THE RULES 'YOUR	'YOUR
HONOUR'	HONOUR'	HONOUR'

THERE IS NO 'EITHER-OR'		NO!
YOU WILL STICK TO THE LAW	THERE IS NO 'EITHER-OR'	AND WE
YOU MUST DO AS YOU ARE TOLD!	WE WON'T DO AS WE ARE TOLD!	WON'T DO AS WE ARE TOLD!

MAYOR. Townspeople and Councillors of this fair city, welcome to you all. I stand before you as your newly-elected Mayor.

The Townspeople display little reaction

Thank you for your support over the last few months … and for your votes of course.

TOWNSPERSON. *(aside)* Well I didn't vote for him.

TOWNSPERSON. *(aside)* He didn't get any support from me.

MAYOR. You have given me the opportunity to wear this glorious necklace for one whole year. It makes me look as magnificent as our beloved statue of the Happy Prince that stands above us here.

TOWNSPERSON. Nothing's as magnificent as the Happy Prince.

The Townspeople murmur in agreement

TOWNSPERSON. A rusty old bath chain can't compare with all that gold and those beautiful gems.

Further agreement from the Townspeople

MAYOR. The Happy Prince has stood watching over our town for a hundred years and, like him, I too will watch over you.

TOWNSPERSON. What, for a hundred years?

The Townspeople laugh

TOWNSPERSON. We've all heard that one before.

MAYOR. In honour of my victory I would like to invite you all, to a celebratory Ball, this Saturday at the Town Hall.

TOWNSPERSON. There'll be a catch, I guarantee it.

MAYOR. And there's another reason for the celebration – my daughter Cecily has just become engaged to Thomas Cardew, son of the richest man in our city and heir to millions.

CECILY. Oh Daddy, I'm not marrying him just for his money!

TOWNSPERSON. Yeh, and she's not marrying him just for his looks neither!

The Townspeople laugh

MAYOR. (*emphatically*) Tickets for the Ball are available from the Town Clerk priced at a very reasonable two guineas each.

TOWNSPEOPLE. Two guineas!

TOWNSPERSON. There's the catch.

TOWNSPERSON. Well, that's the wedding paid for then!

Agreement from the Townspeople

MAYOR. I hope to see you all there. Don't forget to buy your tickets.

CECILY. Oh Daddy, you were marvellous. I do hope everyone comes to my party.

2a EXIT OF MAYOR

The Mayor, the Town Clerk, the Councillors, Cecily & Thomas exit with a flourish

UNDERSCORE

The Townspeople begin to exit

TOWNSPERSON. He's just like all the others, full of himself and only in it for the glory.

TOWNSPERSON. I reckon the voting was rigged, I don't trust those Councillors.

TOWNSPERSON. Well, he's not going to make life any better for us is he?

TEACHER. We must try to make ourselves happy. Look at the Happy Prince. He stands alone but he's not crying.

TOWNSPERSON. I'm glad there's someone in the world who is truly happy.

(Reprise #1) HIGH ABOVE STANDS A STATUE

DREAMY CHILD.

HIGH ABOVE STANDS A STATUE OF A BOY
GOLDEN, BRIGHT, SMILING IN THE SUN
THE HAPPY PRINCE FILLS OUR DAYS WITH HOPE AND
JOY
SHARING HIS LOVE WITH EVERYONE

The Angel appears and observes

UNDERSCORE continues

DREAMY CHILD. I think he looks like an angel.

TEACHER. What nonsense! How do you know what an angel looks like when you've never seen one.

DREAMY CHILD. I do know! I do! I've seen an angel in my dreams.

TEACHER. You children should be far too tired to be dreaming – I can see I shall have to work you even harder. Come along now, back to school.

The Teacher, the School Children and the remaining Townspeople exit

The Angel disappears

Scene 2 **WILL YOU HELP ME? (1) SEAMSTRESS**
(The Town Square & the Seamstress's House)

SONG 3 *I'VE A LONG WAY TO GO*

The Swallow enters the town square hesitantly, looking for a place to sleep. He is carrying a stick with a bundle tied to the end of it

SWALLOW.

NOW THE WINTER IS APPROACHING AND WE
SWALLOWS MUST BE GONE
THE DAYS ARE GETTING SHORTER AND THE NIGHTS
ARE GETTING LONG
I SPENT THE SUMMER BY THE RIVER HAVING SUCH A
LOT OF FUN
BUT IT'S TIME, GOTTA FLY
BETTER LEAVE, SAY GOODBYE
MY LITTLE FEET ARE FREEZING
SO I'M OFF TO FIND THE SUN

I'VE A LONG WAY TO GO
CAN'T GET CAUGHT BY THE SNOW
I'M EXCITED AND LIGHT AS A FEATHER
I'M ON MY WAY TO THE SUN
CHEERIO EVERYONE
TO ESCAPE FROM ALL THIS AWFUL WINTER
WEATHER

I HAVE AN EXPECTATION
THAT MY IMMIGRATION
IS A LONG VACATION
I DESERVE IT!
EGYPT IS MY DESTINATION
(spoken) CAIRO HERE I COME!

(sung) NOW IT'S A LONG WAY TO THE DESERT, SO I
MUST GET UP MY STRENGTH

A THOUSAND MILES OF FLYING IS A HECK OF A
LENGTH
I NEED TO FIND A PLACE TO SPEND THE NIGHT, TO
REST MY WEARY WINGS
THEN IT'S TIME, GOTTA FLY
BETTER LEAVE, SAY GOODBYE
AND I'LL JOIN MY BIRDIE BUDDIES
IN THE VALLEY OF THE KINGS

I'VE A LONG WAY TO GO
CAN'T GET CAUGHT BY THE SNOW
I'M EXCITED AND LIGHT AS A FEATHER
FLYING MILE AFTER MILE
NEED TO SLEEP FOR A WHILE *(yawns)*

The Swallow arrives at the statue of the Happy Prince

Ah! This is the perfect spot for a little kip – a golden
bedroom with plenty of fresh air.

SO I'LL STAY HERE FOR THE NIGHT
CATCH AN EARLY MORNING FLIGHT
AND ESCAPE FROM ALL THIS AWFUL WINTER
WEATHER

*The Swallow sits at the feet of the Happy Prince and a
teardrop falls on his head, represented by a percussion
effect, eg a triangle*

SWALLOW. That's strange, there's not a single cloud in the
sky, the stars are clear and bright and yet it's raining.
(*He starts to lie down and another teardrop falls*) What's the
use of a statue if it can't keep the rain off? I'd better go
and look for a chimney pot. (*He starts to get up and there
is a tinkle of bells as the Happy Prince 'comes to life'. He looks
up and sees the face of the Happy Prince*) Who are you?

HAPPY PRINCE. I am the Happy Prince.

SWALLOW. Well, why are you crying then? Look at me, I'm
soaked through.

HAPPY PRINCE. When I was alive and had a human heart,
I did not know what tears were. I lived in a beautiful
palace where you weren't allowed to be sad.

SWALLOW. Oh yes, where was this palace?

HAPPY PRINCE. Within the old city walls. It was a happy place. Everything around me was so beautiful and I never thought to ask what lay beyond. I was called the Happy Prince and I was happy … if pleasure is happiness.

SWALLOW. Sounds like a great life to me. So how did you end up here?

SONG 4 starts as UNDERSCORE

HAPPY PRINCE. When I died they made a statue of me. They put me up here so high that I can see all the ugliness and misery of the city. And although my heart is now made of lead I cannot stop crying.

SWALLOW. Oh dear, that's terrible. What exactly can you see from up there?

The Seamstress and her Son are seen in their house. The Son is in bed and the Seamstress is sitting embroidering passion flowers onto a ball gown. She is singing to him

SONG 4   LULLABY OF DREAMS

SEAMSTRESS.
EVERY TIME YOU CRY, I'LL SING A LULLABY
SO CLOSE YOUR EYES AND FALL INTO A DREAM
NOTHING CAN MAKE YOU SAD WHEN YOU'RE FAST ASLEEP
IN A WORLD OF TREASURE, YOU'LL FIND PLEASURE
MOUNTAIN-HIGH AND OCEAN-DEEP

UNDERSCORE

HAPPY PRINCE. Far away in a little street there is a house, one of the windows is open and I can see a woman sitting in a chair. Her face is thin and worn and her hands are sore and pricked by needles – she is a seamstress. She is embroidering passion flowers on a satin gown for the Mayor's daughter to wear at the Ball. Her little son is lying beside her. He is ill with a fever.

SONG continues

SEAMSTRESS.

> IN A WORLD OF TREASURE, YOU'LL FIND PLEASURE
> MOUNTAIN-HIGH AND OCEAN-DEEP
> AND YOU CAN COLOUR A RAINBOW IN THE SKY
> AND CATCH A RIDE ON A CLOUD THAT'S PASSING BY
> AND LAUGH WITH LIONS AND BANTER WITH THE BEES
> FLYING HIGH UP ABOVE THE TREES
> AND THERE IS PLENTY FOR EVERYONE TO EAT
> AND THERE ARE SMILES FROM EVERYONE YOU MEET
> AND YOU DO THINGS THAT YOU NEVER DREAMT
> YOU'D DO
> AND ANY WISHES YOU MAKE COME TRUE

> *UNDERSCORE*

SON. Mother, please can I have something to eat? I want an orange.

SEAMSTRESS. My poor darling boy, I have no oranges for you, we have no food at all.

SON. I'm so hot I feel like I'm on fire.

SEAMSTRESS. I will give you river water to help ease your fever. You will soon feel better, my darling. Close your eyes now and try to sleep.

> *SONG continues*

SEAMSTRESS.

> SO EVERY TIME YOU CRY, I'LL SING A LULLABY
> JUST CLOSE YOUR EYES AND FALL INTO A DREAM
> LEAVE ALL YOUR CARES BEHIND WHEN THE DAY IS
> THROUGH
> IF YOU TRUST YOUR DREAM, IT SOON WILL SEEM
> THAT EVERYTHING YOU DREAM COMES TRUE
> CLOSE YOUR EYES, DREAM YOUR DREAMS
> AND EVERYTHING WILL COME TRUE

HAPPY PRINCE. Little Swallow, can you help me? My feet are fixed to this pedestal and I cannot move. Take the ruby from my sword hilt to the poor woman so that she can buy food to make her son better.

SWALLOW. Look … I don't want to appear rude, but I'm

actually on my way to Egypt to join my friends. They'll be having a great time flying up and down the Nile, talking to the large lotus-flowers and sleeping in the tomb of the Great King, Tutankhamen. You should see him, he's all wrapped up in bandages poor thing – but he doesn't smell too bad for someone who's over three thousand years old.

HAPPY PRINCE. Little Swallow. I need your help. Take the ruby to the poor woman.

SWALLOW. Sorry, mate. I don't want to get involved. I'm just going to have a nice little kip and be on my way.

HAPPY PRINCE. Please, little Swallow. Just stay for one night and be my messenger. The boy is so hungry and the mother so sad.

SWALLOW. But I don't even like kids. Last summer, by the river, there were two very rude boys, the miller's sons, who were always throwing stones at me. They never hit me, of course. We swallows fly far too well for that, and besides, I come from a family famous for its agility…

HAPPY PRINCE. (*imploringly*) Little Swallow …

SWALLOW. It's very cold here, you know, and my friends are …

HAPPY PRINCE. (*emphatically*) You must help me.

SWALLOW. (*pause*) Alright then … I'll do it. I'll stay for one night and be your messenger. But I'll be off first thing in the morning.

The Swallow reaches out towards the statue and freezes. There is a tinkling of bells to represent the removal of the ruby from the Happy Prince's sword hilt

The Swallow exits

4a SCENE CHANGE MUSIC

Scene 3　　　　**THE RUBY IS DELIVERED**
　　　　　　　　(The Town Square & the Seamstress's House)

Cecily and Thomas enter the town square. It is night time and the sky is full of stars

THOMAS. (*gazing up at the night sky*) How wonderful the stars are tonight – this surely is the sweetest sight in all the world.

CECILY. Thomas! *I'm* the sweetest sight in all the world – remember!

THOMAS. Of course you are Cecily, how could I forget?

CECILY. I'm not interested in silly stars. All I'm worried about is whether my dress will be ready in time for the Ball.

THOMAS. Cecily, you'll look beautiful in whatever you wear. You'll shine like the stars … um … like the true beauty you are.

CECILY. Not if I can't wear my new dress. I've ordered passion flowers to be embroidered on it, but the seamstress is so lazy and unbelievably slow.

THOMAS. Don't worry, I'm sure she'll finish it in time.

CECILY. But I want to be the Belle of the Ball. (*Glaring at Thomas*) Thomas! Tell me I'll be the Belle of the Ball.

THOMAS. Darling, of course you'll be the …

SONG 5 starts as UNDERSCORE

By jove, look at that amazing bird. It has a beak as red as a ruby. Now what species could that be I wonder?

CECILY. Thomas! You just don't care about me. You're too busy looking at other birds … or clouds … or your wretched stars … Are you going to be like this when we're married? What about my dress?

THOMAS. But darling, this is unbelievable. Just look at that incredible bird shimmering like a crimson comet as it passes through the starlit heavens.

CECILY. Thomas … my dress!

SONG 5   HOW WONDERFUL THE STARS ARE

THOMAS.
FLOATING, FLYING, GRAVITY DEFYING
SOARING, SWOOPING, GRACEFUL AND LIGHT
WATCH IT, SEE IT
WISH THAT I COULD BE IT
FEEL HOW IT DRAWS YOU INTO THE NIGHT

THOMAS.
HOW WONDERFUL THE STARS ARE

CECILY. Thomas, would you please stop …

THOMAS.
SHINING HIGH ABOVE YOU

CECILY. Just listen to me, Thomas …

THOMAS.
A UNIVERSE OF BEAUTY, AGES OLD

CECILY. Please stop looking at the stars …

THOMAS.
A GALAXY OF DIAMONDS, TO BEHOLD

THOMAS. Cecily, just look!

THOMAS.
THE MAGIC WE ARE FEELING

CECILY. I'm not feeling it …

THOMAS.
COMFORTING, UPLIFTING

CECILY. I wish you were more comforting …

THOMAS.
CAN HOLD US AND PROTECT US FROM THE COLD

CECILY. Thomas, you're impossible! *(she exits)*

THOMAS.
A SKY FULL OF SILVER, A WORLD OF GOLD

Thomas is lost in the moment, then realises that Cecily has gone. He runs after her

THOMAS. Cecily, wait!

Townspeople enter (not the School Children)

UNDERSCORE continues

TEACHER. I've never seen a bird like that before. Remarkable! What could it be? I must bring my pupils out tomorrow, I want to make sure they see it.

TOWNSPERSON. It must be a sign of better things to come.

TOWNSPERSON. Maybe our luck's going to change.

TOWNSPERSON. It's certainly as bright as any star I've ever seen.

SONG continues

HAPPY PRINCE.
>FLY LITTLE SWALLOW
>FLY THROUGH THE NIGHT
>TRY LITTLE SWALLOW
>AND THE FUTURE CAN BE BRIGHT

TOWNSPEOPLE (A).
>HOW WONDERFUL THE STARS ARE

TOWNSPEOPLE (B).
>HOW WONDERFUL THE STARS ARE

TOWNSPEOPLE (A).
>SHINING HIGH ABOVE YOU

TOWNSPEOPLE (B).
>SHINING HIGH ABOVE YOU

ALL.
>A UNIVERSE OF BEAUTY, AGES OLD
>A GALAXY OF DIAMONDS, TO BEHOLD

TOWNSPEOPLE (A).
>THE MAGIC WE ARE FEELING

TOWNSPEOPLE (B).
>THE MAGIC WE ARE FEELING

TOWNSPEOPLE (A).
>COMFORTING, UPLIFTING

TOWNSPEOPLE (B).
>COMFORTING, UPLIFTING

ALL.

> CAN HOLD US AND PROTECT US FROM THE COLD
> A SKY FULL OF SILVER, A HEAVENLY WONDER, A
> WORLD OF GOLD

> *The Angel appears and observes*

> *UNDERSCORE continues*

> *The Seamstress is asleep, slumped over her needlework*

SON. Mother, Mother, wake up.

> *The Seamstress wakes, yawning and goes to him*

SEAMSTRESS. What is it my child?

SON. I had a strange dream. I dreamt that a bird was fanning my head with its wings. And now I feel much cooler … I must be getting better.

SEAMSTRESS. Come on now. Sleep little one, sleep.

> *She tucks him in, returns to her needlework and finds the ruby. She goes to the open window to see who might have brought it to her*

> *SONG continues*

TOWNSPEOPLE.

> HOW WONDERFUL THE STARS ARE
> SHINING HIGH ABOVE YOU
> A UNIVERSE OF BEAUTY, AGES OLD
> A GALAXY OF DIAMONDS, TO BEHOLD

TOWNSPEOPLE/SEAMSTRESS/SON.

> THE MAGIC WE ARE FEELING
> COMFORTING, UPLIFTING
> CAN HOLD US AND PROTECT US FROM THE COLD
> A SKY FULL OF SILVER, A HEAVENLY WONDER, A
> WORLD OF GOLD

> *The Townspeople, Seamstress & Son exit*

> *The Angel disappears*

> *UNDERSCORE*

> *The Swallow stands beside the Happy Prince*

SWALLOW. Do you know what? Even though it's still so cold, I feel quite warm now.

HAPPY PRINCE. That is because you have done a good deed.

SWALLOW. Hmm ... I suppose I did. Yes ... put like that. (*Dropping off to sleep*) A good deed ... hmm ...

Scene 4   **ORNITHOLOGY LESSON**
              (The Town Square)

*The following morning in the town square. The Mayor
enters in a huff, with the Town Clerk close behind him.
They are followed in hot pursuit by the Councillors.
During the scene, the Town Clerk is keen to protect the
Mayor from their pestering*

COUNCILLORS. (*assorted pleas to the Mayor*) But your Honour!
Wait! Come back! We have more questions! etc

MAYOR. Stop pestering me! Always so many questions.
Haven't you got better things to do?

COUNCILLOR. But your Honour, with respect, the townspeople are getting restless.

MAYOR. And I'm getting bored.

COUNCILLOR. They're asking for cleaner streets.

MAYOR. Well you know where the brooms are kept.

COUNCILLOR. They're crying out for a park for the children to play in.

MAYOR. Well go and plant a tree.

COUNCILLOR. They want to know when the hospital will
be built.

MAYOR. When it's finished. What a ridiculous question.

COUNCILLOR. And what you're going to do for the poor
people.

MAYOR. You just don't get it do you? Any spare money goes
towards the Ball. Once my daughter is married into
the Cardew fortune, I'll be able to give some away. An
orange at Christmas should be enough to keep them
quiet.

COUNCILLOR. But, your Honour …

TOWN CLERK. I think his Honour has had more than
enough questions for one day.

MAYOR. (*glaring at the Town Clerk*) Thank you, Town Clerk. I'm quite capable of dealing with this myself.

TOWN CLERK. I'm sorry, your Honour, but I thought …

MAYOR. Oh good Lord, here comes that crazy teacher. If she sees me she'll go on at length about the state of her dreadful school. I'm off.

The Mayor exits, followed closely by the Town Clerk

COUNCILLOR. (*calling after him*) But your Honour. What *about* education?

The Councillors exit continuing to ask the Mayor questions. The Teacher enters cautiously with the School Children, searching for the unusual bird that was seen the night before

TEACHER. Now quietly children, we don't want to scare him away.

CHILD. (*aside*) She's more likely to scare it than we are.

The School Children laugh

TEACHER. Ssh! I said quietly! Now this is exactly where I was last night when I saw the unusual bird.

CHILD. What did it look like, Miss?

TEACHER. It was small … well, small-ish. Although, I think it was quite large … for a small bird.

CHILD. What colour was it, Miss?

TEACHER. It was black … but then it was a dark night. Or was it white? … I didn't have the right glasses on.

CHILD. Miss … was it like that bird up there?

TEACHER. That's it! That's it exactly! I knew it would be around here somewhere. Let's take a closer look. (*She looks through the wrong end of the binoculars*) Goodness me, I was right. It's an absolute tiddler. A wren perhaps.

EARNEST. Miss … you've got the binoculars round the wrong way.

The School Children laugh

TEACHER. Ah, yes. Well done, Earnest. Just testing. (*She* *looks through other end of the binoculars*). Hmm … how very interesting.

EARNEST. Miss … could it be the species Hirundo rustica on account of its long pointed wings and unusually notched or forked tail?

TEACHER. What are you saying Earnest? Please do not speak in riddles. It is most unbecoming in a child of your stature.

EARNEST. It looks like a bird from the family Hirundinidae or swallow, to give it its common name.

TEACHER. A swallow? In the middle of winter? Really Earnest, if you must make suggestions, please do think before you speak. We all know that the swallow is a migratory bird that leaves our shores for warmer countries long before the weather turns cold. No, no. This little chap is much more rare.

SONG 6   BIRD SONG

TEACHER.
> THERE ARE MANY KINDS OF BIRD I COULD MENTION
> THERE ARE LOTS OF DIFFERENT TYPES I COULD NAME
> THERE ARE PRETTY ONES WHO GRAB YOUR ATTENTION
> THERE ARE OTHERS WHO ARE REALLY RATHER PLAIN
> THERE'S A FUNNY CHAP YOU HEAR IN THE SPRING
> AND A SKYLARK TRILLING HIGH ON THE WING
> I'M AN EXPERT IN THIS FIELD
> IT'S A SKILL I HAVE CONCEALED
> BUT I'M BLOWED IF I CAN NAME THIS 'THING'!

TEACHER.
> NOW WAIT A MINUTE

SCHOOL CHILDREN.
> WE'RE WAITING, WE'RE WAITING

TEACHER.
> I THINK I'VE GOT IT

SCHOOL CHILDREN.

SHE'S THINKING, SHE'S THINKING

TEACHER.

I'M POSITIVELY, DEFINITELY, SUPER-SEMI-
ABSOLUTELY PRETTY SURE
I MAY HAVE FOUND A CLUE

SCHOOL CHILDREN.

SHE MAY HAVE FOUND A CLUE

TEACHER.

I CAN'T BE CERTAIN

SCHOOL CHILDREN.

SHE CANNOT BE CERTAIN

TEACHER.

OF WHAT WE HAVE HERE

SCHOOL CHILDREN.

SHE'S DOUBTING, SHE'S DOUBTING

TEACHER.

BUT CERTAIN INDICATIONS LEAD ME TO BELIEVE
THAT WHAT WE HAVE HERE MAKE ME THINK THAT
WHAT I THINK IS TRUE

SCHOOL CHILDREN.

MIGHT BE TRUE, MIGHT BE TRUE
PLEASE TELL US DO

TEACHER.

TAKE A PEAK AT HIS BEAK, IT IS LONG AND IT IS
SLEEK
IT IS TOTALLY UNIQUE IN EVERY WAY
YOU WILL NOTE THAT THE THROAT ON THE
UNDERSIDE IS RED
I SUGGEST, FROM HIS CHEST, HE IS CLEARLY OVER-FED
HE'S A GREEDY LITTLE FELLOW I WOULD SAY

SCHOOL CHILDREN.

GREEDY SHE WOULD SAY, GREEDY SHE WOULD SAY

TEACHER.

I'VE STUDIED ORNITHOLOGY, WITH HONOURS IN
GEOLOGY
I'D LIKE TO TELL YOU MORE IF YOU CAN FOLLOW

SCHOOL CHILDREN.
> SHE THINKS SHE'S AN AUTHORITY, BUT SHE'S IN THE MINORITY
> IT'S CLEAR TO US WE'RE LOOKING AT A SWALLOW

TEACHER. I hope you're all paying attention – there will be a short test later. And if you listen you might learn something.

TEACHER.
> NOW IT COULD BE A THRUSH, BUT I'M CAREFUL NOT TO RUSH
> FOR IT MIGHT BE MORE AQUATIC – LIKE A GREBE
> OR A HAWK OR A STORK, YELLOWHAMMER OR AN OWL
> OR A WREN OR A HEN OR A TYPE OF GUINEA-FOWL
> OR THE LESSER-SPOTTED PUFFIN FROM ANTIBES

SCHOOL CHILDREN.
> PUFFIN FROM ANTIBES, PUFFIN FROM ANTIBES

TEACHER.
> I LEARNT AT UNIVERSITY OF AVIAN DIVERSITY
> FORGIVE ME, BUT I AM INCLINED TO WALLOW

SCHOOL CHILDREN.
> SHE'S TOTALLY UNSHAKEABLE, THIS BIRD IS UNMISTAKABLE
> IT'S CERTAIN THAT WE'RE LOOKING AT A SWALLOW

TEACHER.
> IT MIGHT BE A KITE, YES I'M SURE I AM RIGHT

SCHOOL CHILDREN.
> BUT A KITE HAS A WHITER BACK

TEACHER.
> I'D SAY IT'S A JAY, FOR ITS FEATHERS ARE GREY

SCHOOL CHILDREN.
> WELL YOU'RE WRONG, 'CAUSE A SWALLOW'S BLACK

TEACHER.
> NOW IT MUST BE A FINCH AND I WILL NOT BUDGE AN INCH
> THOUGH A NIGHTINGALE WOULD BETTER FIT THE BILL

OR A TERN OR A TIT, EITHER BEARDED, GREAT OR
BLUE
OR A FRAIL KIND OF QUAIL, OR A TINY COCKATOO
OR THE GREATER-CRESTED PARROT FROM BRAZIL

SCHOOL CHILDREN.

PARROT FROM BRAZIL, PARROT FROM BRAZIL

TEACHER.

AND NOW I'LL MAKE MY CHOICE AND THEN WE CAN
REJOICE
JUST THINK HOW FAMOUS I WILL BE!

SCHOOL CHILDREN.

SHE CLEARLY HASN'T HEARD, WE'VE IDENTIFIED
THE BIRD

TEACHER.

TO PROVE I'M RIGHT, I'LL TAKE A LOOK
AND SEE WHAT'S WRITTEN IN MY BOOK
AH! HERE WE ARE, PAGE THIRTY-THREE
SEE ITEM TEN, APPENDIX B

The Teacher consults her text book

TEACHER. Appendix B, item ten.

*She looks at the Swallow, then at the book. She removes
her glasses and looks again at the Swallow, then at the
book*

TEACHER. (*confidently*) As I thought. A swallow!

6a EXIT

The Teacher and the School Children exit

Scene 5   **WILL YOU HELP ME? (2) THE WRITER**
(The Town Square & the Writer's Attic)

The Swallow wakes up

SWALLOW. Right, I'm off. Anything you want from Egypt? A little wooden replica of the Great Pyramid perhaps? A Tutankhamen tea towel? Or maybe some preserved camel dung? (*Pause*) Makes a great paper weight you know!

HAPPY PRINCE. Little Swallow, will you not stay with me for one more night?

SWALLOW. Oh, here you go again. I keep telling you, my friends are waiting for me in Egypt. I'm missing all the fun. They'll be visiting the sphinx, bathing in the warm waters of the Nile and feasting on tasty titbits fit for a Pharoah. Sorry, mate. I'm off. And besides, I'll freeze to death if I stay here any longer – I haven't got my thermals on.

HAPPY PRINCE. Little Swallow, far away across the city I see a young man in an attic.

6b UNDERSCORE starts

The Writer is seen in his attic sitting at a desk with a candle, holding a quill pen and trying to write. Dying embers are burning in the fire grate and beside it is an empty wood basket. He is cold and hungry

He is hunched over a desk covered with papers trying to finish a play that will earn him the money he desperately needs. He is too cold to write any more, there is barely any fire in the grate and hunger has made him faint.

WRITER. (*as he writes*) Scene two … A large and lovely garden with soft, green grass. The garden is full of

flowers … and peach trees… heavy with blossoms of …
*(He puts down his pen and rubs his hands together to warm
them. He shivers, stands up and moves around to try and
keep warm. Sitting again)* … with delicate blossoms of …
Oh, it's no use, I'm so hungry I can't think.

There is a knock at the door

WRITER. Come in.

The Town Clerk enters. He is carrying a lantern

SONG 7 starts as UNDERSCORE

WRITER. Oh! Town Clerk.

TOWN CLERK. Good evening to you. Where is the play?

WRITER. Er … the play… yes, of course. I'm afraid …
um …

TOWN CLERK. Rehearsals were due to begin yesterday,
you've had long enough to finish it. The Schoolteacher
needs as much time as possible to rehearse with the
children.

WRITER. Please forgive me, Town Clerk, but I'm finding it
rather …

    *SONG 7   WHERE'S THE PLAY? / HOW CAN I
                      WRITE?*

TOWN CLERK.

I AM HERE ON BEHALF OF THE MAYOR
FOR THE PLAY YOU ARE WRITING IS OVERDUE
YOU ARE TAKING SO LONG, WHAT IS GOING ON?
DON'T FORGET AN AGREEMENT WAS MADE

IT APPEARS THAT YOU HAVEN'T A CARE
FOR YOU SIT AND DO NOTHING THE WHOLE DAY
THROUGH
YOU ARE LAZY AND SLOW AND YOU OUGHT TO
KNOW
IT IS LIKELY THAT YOU WON'T BE PAID!

WRITER.

HOW CAN I WRITE WHEN I'M HUNGRY?

HOW CAN I WRITE WHEN MY HANDS ARE COLD?
THERE IS NO FIRE TO WARM ME
NOTHING AT ALL TO FEED MY SOUL

TOWN CLERK.
I WON'T HEAR ANY EXCUSES FROM YOU
THEY HAVE NO EFFECT AS A RULE

WRITER.
WHAT D'YOU EXPECT ME TO DO?

TOWN CLERK.
YOU'RE A FOOL! SUCH A FOOL!

WRITER.
WITHOUT MONEY I CANNOT BUY FOOD
WITHOUT FOOD I AM FADING AWAY
AND HUNGER HAS DARKENED MY MOOD

TOWN CLERK.
WHERE'S THE PLAY? WHERE'S THE PLAY?

TOWN CLERK. This is turning into a complete farce. If this play isn't ready in time to perform at the Mayor's Ball on Saturday he'll have my guts for garters. And I shall personally see to it that you don't receive a single penny.

SONG continues

WRITER.
HOW CAN I LOOK TO THE FUTURE?
THERE MAY BE THINGS I DON'T WANT TO SEE
IS THIS THE PATH I HAVE CHOSEN?
OR IS THIS THE WAY IT HAS TO BE?

TOWN CLERK.
I WON'T TAKE ANY MORE NONSENSE FROM YOU
MY INSTRUCTIONS ARE BEING IGNORED

WRITER.
SO WHAT D'YOU EXPECT ME TO DO?

TOWN CLERK.
YOU'RE A FRAUD! SUCH A FRAUD!

WRITER.
IF YOU GIVE ME SOME CASH IN ADVANCE

AND ALLOW ME A LITTLE MORE TIME

THEN YOU'LL GIVE THIS POOR WRITER A CHANCE

TOWN CLERK.

IT'S A CRIME! SUCH A CRIME!

TOWN CLERK.	**WRITER.**
IT APPEARS THAT YOU	
HAVEN'T A CARE	HOW CAN I WRITE
FOR YOU SIT AND DO	WHEN I'M
NOTHING THE	HUNGRY?
WHOLE DAY THROUGH	HOW CAN I WRITE
YOU ARE LAZY AND SLOW	WHEN MY
AND YOU OUGHT TO KNOW	HANDS ARE COLD?
IT IS LIKELY THAT YOU	I CANNOT GO
WON'T	ON
BE PAID!	
YOU WILL DO WHAT	AND FINISH THE PLAY
I SAY	
WRITE THE PLAY!	I CANNOT GO ON

TOWN CLERK. I will give you until tomorrow. I will be here at noon to collect the finished play. You won't receive a penny until then. Good Evening to you.

The Town Clerk exits

The Writer buries his head in his hands in desperation

SWALLOW. Well … it did feel good helping that poor woman and her son. (*Pause*) Alright … I'll stay one more night. Shall I take a ruby to the Writer?

HAPPY PRINCE. Alas, I have no ruby now. My eyes are all that I have left. They are made of rare sapphires, brought out of India a thousand years ago. Pluck one out and take it to him.

SWALLOW. (*sadly*) Dear Prince, I can't do that to you.

HAPPY PRINCE. Little Swallow, do as I ask. He will sell it to the jeweller and buy food and firewood and be able to finish his play.

SONG 7a FLY LITTLE SWALLOW

The Swallow reaches out towards the statue and freezes. There is a tinkling of bells to represent the removal of a sapphire from one of the Happy Prince's eyes

The Swallow exits

HAPPY PRINCE.
FLY LITTLE SWALLOW
FLY THROUGH THE NIGHT
TRY LITTLE SWALLOW
AND THE FUTURE CAN BE BRIGHT

UNDERSCORE continues

The Writer still has his head buried in his hands and slowly looks up as he speaks

WRITER. I'll never finish my play on time. I'm ruined. There must be something left to eat, or some wood to burn.

The Angel appears and observes. The Writer tries to warm his hands over the dying embers and looks for wood in the log basket. There is none there but he finds the sapphire

What's this? How did it get here? (*He takes it over to the candle*) It looks like … a sapphire!

7b UNDERSCORE starts

It can't be … can it? This must be from a great admirer – someone who actually appreciates my work. Now I'll be able to finish my play.

The Writer exits but the Angel remains. The Dreamy Child enters the town square and walks over to the Happy Prince. She stands staring at the statue. The Angel stands staring at the Child

(Reprise #2) HIGH ABOVE STANDS A STATUE

DREAMY CHILD.
HIGH ABOVE STANDS A STATUE OF A BOY
GOLDEN, BRIGHT, SMILING IN THE SUN
THE HAPPY PRINCE FILLS OUR DAYS WITH HOPE AND
JOY …

The Dreamy Child turns round slowly and gasps as she sees the Angel. She walks slowly towards him. When the Angel realises that he can be seen he exits hastily. The Dreamy Child stands for a second, frozen in amazement, turns and exits excitedly

If an interval is required this is where it should be. If there is no interval the Angel re-enters almost immediately to start Scene 6

Scene 6	ANGEL/MAYOR/TOWNSPEOPLE CROSSOVER

(The Town Square)

The Angel enters slightly flustered. He stands isolated in a spotlight and is speaking on his mobile phone

ANGEL. Hello … hello … yes, hello … aaagh … *press 1 for Revelations, 2 for Miracles, 3 for Last Judgements or 4 to speak to an operator* … right, 4. (*He presses the keypad*) Hello, yes it's Angel 4962 here. Can you hear me? Sorry, you're breaking up a bit. Can you tell God I'm having trouble finding anything precious for him down here, it's a bit confusing and I think I need some help. Well, is he there? … Can I speak to him? … He's playing golf?! … Well what am I supposed to be looking for?... Do you have any suggestions? … Look, there's someone coming, I've got to go … I think people can see me.

The Angel exits

SONG 8 starts as UNDERSCORE

The Mayor enters with the Councillors (not the Town Clerk)

MAYOR. What do you mean, no one's bought a ticket yet?

COUNCILLOR. With respect, your Honour, I think that two guineas is perhaps a little steep for most people in our town.

MAYOR. A little steep! Do speak English! Hills are steep, steeples are steep – two guineas for a ticket to the Ball of the year is quite frankly not steep. In fact it's positively … flat! *(He exits laughing at his joke)*

COUNCILLORS. *(following the Mayor)* But, your Honour! … Wait your Honour! etc

*The Match Girl, several Townspeople and a small group
of children, including the Dreamy Child, enter*

TOWNSPERSON 1. I'm not paying two guineas to prance
around all night with the likes of Mr Mayor and his
cronies.

TOWNSPERSON 2. But my dear, it would be a night to
remember.

TOWNSPERSON 1. Yes … and so was the Fire of London.
Which reminds me … (*To the Match Girl*) box of
matches please, love.

MATCH GIRL. Here you are, Sir. That's a penny please.

She takes a penny from the Townsperson

TOWNSPERSON 2. I can't believe the price of matches these
days.

The Townspeople move to exit

CHILD. I don't believe you. You're lying.

DREAMY CHILD. No I'm not. I did see one.

CHILD. No you didn't. You're making it up.

DREAMY CHILD. He was an angel I tell you. I know what
they look like.

CHILD. Liar, liar, your hair's on fire!

DREAMY CHILD. Leave me alone, I know what I saw.

The Dreamy Child walks away defiantly

CHILD. Come on, let's get her.

*The Dreamy Child is chased by the other children. They
run circles round the Match Girl, then exit noisily*

Scene 7 **WILL YOU HELP ME? (3) MATCH GIRL**
(The Town Square continued)

MATCH GIRL. Matches! Penny a box!

SONG 8 *MATCHES FOR SALE*

MATCH GIRL.
MATCHES FOR SALE
MATCHES FOR SALE
LOVELY AND DRY
GIVE THEM A TRY
PLEASE STOP AND BUY
MATCHES FOR SALE

PENNY A BOX
PENNY A BOX
CHEAP AS CAN BE
YOU WILL AGREE
BUY THEM FROM ME
MATCHES FOR SALE

WHY MUST LIFE BE SO LONELY
WORKING DAY AFTER DAY?
I'D BE HAPPY IF ONLY
I COULD FIND ANOTHER WAY

The Angel appears and observes. He is a little more discreet this time, aware that he may be noticed

PENNY A BOX
PENNY A BOX
CHEAP AS CAN BE
YOU WILL AGREE
BUY THEM FROM ME
MATCHES FOR SALE

UNDERSCORE continues

The Town Clerk enters

TOWN CLERK. *(ticking off his list of things to organise for the Ball)* Banner, yes … Cecily's dress … the play, urrggh, the wretched play. *(Noticing the Match Girl)*…Ah yes, matches. Child, which are your best matches?

MATCH GIRL. They're all the same Sir, penny a box. Best your money can buy.

TOWN CLERK. Well the last ones I bought were damp. How do I know that these ones won't be?

MATCH GIRL. My father and I cut and packed them all ourselves, Sir. I can assure you our matches are always lovely and dry.

TOWN CLERK. *(Giving her three pennies)* In that case, I'll have three boxes.

MATCH GIRL. Yes, Sir. Thank you, Sir. *(Handing him the matches)* There you are, Sir.

TOWN CLERK. And they'd better not be damp or I'll make sure that you and your father go out of business.

The Town Clerk exits

SONG continues

MATCH GIRL.

WHY MUST LIFE BE SO LONELY
WORKING DAY AFTER DAY?
I'D BE HAPPY IF ONLY
I COULD FIND ANOTHER WAY

MATCHES FOR SALE
MATCHES FOR SALE

The Dreamy Child rushes on still being chased by the other children

LOVELY AND DRY
GIVE THEM A TRY
PLEASE STOP AND BUY …

The School Children knock into the Match Girl's tray and her match boxes fall to the ground. The School Children run off and the Match Girl kneels down to pick up her matches

MATCHES FOR SALE

The Angel disappears

Lights up on the Swallow and the Happy Prince

SWALLOW. Well, HP. I've come to say goodbye.

HAPPY PRINCE. Little Swallow, will you not stay with me for one more night?

SWALLOW. One more night! That's the third time you've asked me. Look, I took your ruby to the poor seamstress, one of your eyes to the penniless writer and now I'm off. It's winter and the snow will be here soon. It's lovely in Egypt at this time of year – I'd take you with me if you weren't stuck up here. Tell you what, I'll bring you back a nice new ruby and a sapphire as blue as the Great Sea. I'll half inch one from somewhere.

The Happy Prince looks questioningly at the Swallow

SWALLOW. Half inch – you know, pinch.

SONG 8a starts as UNDERSCORE

HAPPY PRINCE. In the square below sits a little match girl. Her matches have fallen in the gutter and they are all ruined. Her father will beat her if she does not bring home any money and she is crying. She has no shoes or stockings and her little head is bare. Pluck out my other eye and give it to her and her father will not beat her.

SWALLOW. (*pause*) Alright. I'll stay with you for one more night. But I'm not going to pluck out your other eye or you'll be completely blind.

The Happy Prince looks imploringly at the Swallow

SWALLOW. Fair enough, you win… I can see I'll be bringing you back two sapphires.

The Swallow reaches out towards the statue and freezes. There is a tinkling of bells to represent the removal of the other sapphire from the Happy Prince

The Swallow exits

SONG 8a   (Reprise) MATCHES FOR SALE

HAPPY PRINCE.

FLY LITTLE SWALLOW
FLY THROUGH THE NIGHT
TRY LITTLE SWALLOW
AND THE FUTURE CAN BE BRIGHT

The Match Girl becomes transfixed by one particular box of matches which she picks up and studies carefully. She opens it and discovers the sapphire

SONG continues

The Match Girl is now optimistic as she sings

MATCH GIRL.

LOVELY AND DRY
GIVE THEM A TRY
PLEASE STOP AND BUY
MATCHES FOR SALE

The Match Girl runs off excitedly

Scene 8	**WILL YOU HELP ME? (4) GOLD FROM HEAVEN**
	(The Town Square)

HAPPY PRINCE. Little Swallow, it is time for you to go.

SWALLOW. How can I leave you now? You're completely blind.

HAPPY PRINCE. But Swallow, the wind is now blowing from the north and the snow will be here very soon.

SWALLOW. (*to himself, sadly*) It's already too late. I'd never make it to Egypt now. (*Pause*) I'm going to stay right here and tell you exciting stories about all the places I've visited. About the red ibises on the banks of the Nile, the Sphinx, who lives in the desert and the great green snake that sleeps in a palm tree.

HAPPY PRINCE. Dear little Swallow. You tell me about so many marvellous things, but what saddens me is the suffering of men and women. Look around my city, little Swallow and tell me what you see.

SONG 9 starts as UNDERSCORE

The Townspeople (including the School Children) begin to enter and create a tableau of what the Swallow is describing

SWALLOW. I can see rich people in their beautiful houses and beggars sitting outside their gates. I can see worried townspeople and the sad looks on the faces of hungry children. Under the archway of a bridge two small boys are lying huddled together trying to keep warm.

HAPPY PRINCE. I am covered with fine gold, you must take it off leaf by leaf and give it to the poor people of my city. The living always think that gold can make them happy. Take it to them, then you are free to go.

The Swallow reaches out towards the statue and freezes.
There is a tinkling of bells and the light on the Happy
Prince fades to represent the removal of his gold leaf

The Swallow exits

TOWNSPERSON 1. D'you know, those look like snow clouds to me.

TOWNSPERSON 2. No, that'll just be a bit of a shower I reckon.

TOWNSPERSON 1. Yes, but the wind's blowing from the north and that always means snow.

TOWNSPERSON 2. It's just rain I tell you.

TOWNSPERSON 1. Well it certainly feels cold enough to snow.

CHILD. We can build a snowman.

CHILD. Yes! And go skating on the river.

TOWNSPERSON. I don't know why you're so happy, there's another hard winter ahead. How are we going to get through it with all that snow?

TOWNSPERSON. Be quiet you lot, all you ever talk about is the weather.

TOWNSPERSON. If you're that worried about the winter, push off to somewhere warmer.

TOWNSPERSON. Yes, like Iceland!

They laugh raucously

CHILD. Hey look! It's snowing.

CHILD. S/he's right! It's snowing.

TOWNSPERSON. That ain't snow, it's the wrong colour.

TOWNSPERSON. Then it must be rain.

TOWNSPERSON. It looks like gold.

TOWNSPERSON. How can it be gold?

TOWNSPERSON. It *is* gold.

TOWNSPERSON. Where's it coming from?

TOWNSPERSON. Up there.

TOWNSPERSON. It's incredible.

TOWNSPERSON. It's coming from heaven.

DREAMY CHILD. It's from the angel!

The crowd speak all at once – enthusiastic cries of joy and delight at their good fortune

A few leaves of gold float gently down from above onto the crowd as the Townspeople sing

SONG 9   GOLDEN LEAVES

TOWNSPEOPLE.
SEE IT FALLING
DAZZLING, ENTHRALLING
TWISTING, TURNING
GRACEFUL AND LIGHT
WATCH IT GLEAMING
MAYBE WE ARE DREAMING
FEEL HOW IT DRAWS YOU INTO THE NIGHT

The Swallow enters and circles the crowd. Leaves of gold continue to fall as if being dropped by the Swallow. The Townspeople gather them up

HAPPY PRINCE.	SCHOOL CHILDREN.	TOWNSPEOPLE (A) & (B).
FLY LITTLE	GOLDEN	
SWALLOW	LEAVES ARE	
FLY THROUGH	FALLING	
THE NIGHT	DOWN FROM	
TRY LITTLE	HEAVEN.	
SWALLOW		
AND THE		
FUTURE CAN BE	FALLING	
BRIGHT	DOWN FROM	THE
	HEAVEN	MAGIC WE ARE
		FEELING
FLY		(THE MAGIC WE
LITTLE	FROM	ARE FEELING)
SWALLOW	HEAVEN	COMFORTING,
		UPLIFTING
FLY		(COMFORTING,
LITTLE	FROM	UPLIFTING)
SWALLOW	HEAVEN	CAN HOLD US
		AND PROTECT US
FLY LITTLE		FROM THE COLD
SWALLOW	A SKY FULL OF	A SKY FULL OF
FLY LITTLE	SILVER,	SILVER,
SWALLOW	A HEAVENLY	A HEAVENLY
FLY LITTLE	WONDER	WONDER,
SWALLOW	A WORLD	A WORLD
LITTLE SWALLOW	OF	OF
FLY	GOLD	GOLD

Ever more golden leaves continue to fall and are gathered up gleefully by the Townspeople

TOWNSPEOPLE.

GOLDEN LEAVES FALLING FROM THE SKY ABOVE
CAN'T BELIEVE WHAT WE SEE IS TRUE
IT'S NEVER BEEN SEEN, JUST LOOK AT IT GLEAM
THERE'S PLENTY FOR ME AND YOU
THIS ISN'T A DREAM, WHAT CAN IT ALL MEAN?

The music comes to an abrupt halt and the golden leaves stop falling. The Townspeople freeze in tableau. The lights go down on them and they exit

The Angel appears and observes

SONG 9a starts as UNDERSCORE

The Swallow makes his way slowly back to the Happy Prince

HAPPY PRINCE. Thank you my friend, thank you. Your work here is done, now you must leave me.

SWALLOW. (*kisses the statue*) I can't leave you now. I will stay with you forever.

SONG 9a   (Reprise) I'VE A LONG WAY TO GO

SWALLOW.
I'VE A LONG WAY TO GO
CAN'T GET CAUGHT BY THE SNOW ...
FLYING MILE AFTER MILE
NEED TO SLEEP FOR A WHILE ...

The Swallow places a dead bird at the Happy Prince's feet to represent himself and exits slowly

As the Swallow exits, the Happy Prince slowly bows his head and places both hands on his heart. There is a final tinkle of bells to represent his heart breaking. The light on him dims further

The Angel disappears

The Mayor, the Town Clerk and the Town Councillors enter

MAYOR. So ... does anyone know what all the commotion was about last night?

COUNCILLOR. No, your Honour. But apparently some kind of miracle took place.

MAYOR. Miracle? Miracles don't happen around here. At least not without my permission.

COUNCILLOR. No, your Honour. But unusual things have been going on lately.

MAYOR. I don't know what's going on here these days. (*Noticing the statue*) Even the Happy Prince looks shabby.

COUNCILLOR. Yes, your Honour. Very shabby indeed, your Honour.

MAYOR. The ruby has fallen out of his sword, his eyes are missing and he is no longer covered with gold. In fact, he's little better than a beggar.

COUNCILLOR. Yes, your Honour. Little better than a beggar, your Honour.

MAYOR. And there's even a dead bird at his feet. We really must issue a proclamation that birds are not allowed to die here.

COUNCILLORS. (*in unison*) No, your Honour. Not allowed to die here, your Honour.

MAYOR. As he's no longer beautiful, he's no longer useful. Take it down immediately and melt it in the furnace. We'll use the metal to build another statue and it will be a statue of ... me!

TOWN CLERK. (*shocked*) Of *you*, Sir?

The Councillors and the Mayor look at the Town Clerk in disbelief

TOWN CLERK. (*changing his tone*) Of you, Sir.

MAYOR. And get rid of that blasted bird. Throw it on the rubbish heap where it belongs.

TOWN CLERK. Yes, your Honour. Of course, your Honour. If I may say, your Honour, you are actually running a little late. You're making the opening speech at the Ball at eight o'clock ... your Honour.

MAYOR. (*to the Town Clerk*) All right, all right. Stop fussing.

He picks on one of the Town Councillors

Now you, make sure my instructions are carried out to the letter. Take the statue to the furnace immediately and dispose of that infernal bird.

COUNCILLOR. Yes, your Honour. Of course, your Honour.

MAYOR. The rest of you, follow me. We have a Ball to attend.

The Mayor, the Town Clerk and the Councillors exit, leaving the unfortunate Councillor on stage who contemplates how to remove the statue

9b SCENE CHANGE MUSIC

The Happy Prince exits

To cover the exit of the Happy Prince and the scene change into the Ballroom, the remaining golden leaves are swept away by a couple of Townspeople whistling merrily. Downstage of this, the Town Clerk is collecting tickets from the Townspeople as they arrive and queue for the Ball.

TOWN CLERK. (*taking the tickets*) Good evening madam, thank you sir. Have a lovely evening... etc

Scene 9   **THE MAYOR'S BALL**
(The Ballroom at the Town Hall)

The scene opens with the closing moment from the Writer's new play which is being performed by the Teacher and the School Children at the Mayor's Ball. The Guests (Townspeople) are watching, as are the Mayor, the Town Clerk, the Councillors, Thomas and Cecily

In the play, the 'Giant' played by a child, is standing on the plinth (vacated by the Happy Prince). He is wearing a false beard and a long costume that reaches right down to the floor to make him appear taller. A 'small boy' dressed in white stands beside him

TEACHER. (*as the Narrator*) And the child smiled on the Giant and said to him …

CHILD. (*as the Small Boy*) You let me play once in your garden. Today you shall come with me to my garden which is Paradise.

The Giant lies down. The School Children form a semicircle behind him. They throw white blossom petals over the Giant

TEACHER. (*as the Narrator*) And when the children ran in that afternoon they found the Giant lying dead under the tree all covered with white blossoms. The End.

The Guests applaud politely. The School Children and the Teacher take a bow

GUESTS. Weren't they good. Well done. Jolly good, etc.

MAYOR. Well done children, Miss Prism. A good attempt at a difficult script. A word Mr Wilde.

WRITER. Yes, Sir.

MAYOR. Not bad Wilde. Not bad. Can't help thinking it might be more effective as a short story.

WRITER. Well, it might have been better if I'd had more time.

TOWN CLERK. If it wasn't for me, your Honour, the play wouldn't have been finished at all.

WRITER. (*to the Town Clerk*) It was nothing to do with you. I had a stroke of luck – I came into a small fortune.

MAYOR. Yes, I heard about the sapphire – quite a mystery really, but lucky for you in the event.

WRITER. Mr Mayor, I've written another play that might be right for next year's Ball. It's a comedy about a baby who is found in a handbag.

MAYOR. A handbag?! Hmm … it might work! Do excuse me, I have to speak to my guests. (*Clearing his throat*) Ladies and Gentlemen. It is indeed a great pleasure to see you all here tonight at my Ball. Ticket sales for tonight went through the roof and broke all previous records – the last minute rush caught us all unawares. I find it most surprising that so many of you could even afford it. Anyway, here you all are and I know you will want to join me in wishing my daughter Cecily and her fiancé an extremely rich - I mean happy - future. So, all that said, let the dancing commence. Have a Ball!

9c DANCE MUSIC (UNDERSCORE)

Some of the Guests (maybe wearing masks) start to dance. The dancing should take place up stage and be fairly gentle so as not to distract from the dialogue

TOWN CLERK. (*introducing the Mayor to various guests*) Your Honour, may I introduce you to your daughter's Seamstress, Mrs Chasuble. And this is her son.

MAYOR. Delighted to see you Mrs … er … and your son looks very well.

SEAMSTRESS. Yes, I've been able to buy him food at last, thanks to the wonderful ruby that I found.

MAYOR. You found a ruby? And the playwright found a sapphire. Hm, how interesting. Well, I must say, you've done a marvellous job on my daughter's gown.

SEAMSTRESS. Thank you, your Honour.

CECILY. Luckily for you it arrived just in time. But, I do look rather beautiful in it. Don't you agree Thomas?

THOMAS. Yes, my darling, you are as radiant as the stars.

CECILY. So you keep saying, you're making me sound like the Milky Way.

THOMAS. Well, the Milky Way is the finest collection of celestial bodies that can be seen with the naked eye.

CECILY. There you go again. I've had just about enough of you and your star-gazing. You have to make a choice – are you going to gaze at the stars or at me?

THOMAS. (*pause, thinking*) Um …

Cecily flounces off to another part of the Ballroom. Thomas purses her and they continue their argument in the background

TOWN CLERK. And this is Mr George Swann and his young daughter. (*Aside to the Mayor*) You know, she's the match girl.

MAYOR. (*aside to the Town Clerk*) What the blazes is a match girl doing here? (*Turning to Mr Swann and his daughter*) Ah! Delighted you could make it. How are things in the match selling business?

MR SWANN. Very well indeed, thank you, Sir. Since we came into our small fortune.

MAYOR. Don't tell me, you found a bag of diamonds in the gutter!

MATCH GIRL. No, I found a sapphire. It was hidden in one of my match boxes.

MR SWANN. So we've bought a shop and have started producing our own brand of matches.

MAYOR. (*aside to Town Clerk*) Why is everyone getting rich, apart from me?!

MR SWANN. I've named the matches in honour of my daughter Vesta, because she found the sapphire.

MAYOR. (*sarcastically*) Ah … really? How interesting. Well I'll instruct Cook to use Vesta matches from now on, Mr Swann.

The Town Councillor who was instructed to remove the statue of the Happy Prince enters and approaches the Mayor

COUNCILLOR. Excuse me your Honour, I've just had word from the foundry.

MAYOR. (*sarcastically*) Don't tell me. They've found four pearl necklaces and a tiara!

COUNCILLOR. No, your Honour. The statue of the Happy Prince has been melted down as per your instructions, but they were left with a broken lead heart. What would you like them to do with it?

MAYOR. A lead heart! What use is that to me? I want precious stones, not defective metal. Throw it out on the rubbish heap along with that dead swallow.

COUNCILLOR. Yes, your Honour. Of course, your Honour.

MAYOR. (*to himself*) Thank goodness I'm marrying my daughter into a wealthy family, otherwise I'd be the poorest man in the city.

CECILY. (*screaming at Thomas*) You horrid man!

UNDERSCORE comes to an abrupt halt

I don't know what I ever saw in you. The wedding is off!

She throws her engagement ring at him and runs off crying. The crowd gasp. Thomas follows her

THOMAS. Cecily! Darling, come back!

Thomas exits

MAYOR. The wedding is off?! What on earth? … Where are you two going? … Come back! (*Burying his head in his hands*) I'm ruined.

TOWN CLERK. Excuse me, your Honour.

MAYOR. (*impatiently*) What now?!

TOWN CLERK. I was just wondering…

MAYOR. (*suspiciously*) Yes …?

TOWN CLERK. (*tentatively*) Would you like the next dance?

MAYOR. (*furiously*) Keep your hands off me!

The Mayor exits dramatically pursued by the Town Clerk. The other Councillors take the opportunity to join in with the festivities

SONG 10   WHEN YOUR DREAM IS IN SIGHT

ALL.

DANCE A LITTLE DANCE
AND STEP INTO THE LIGHT
THE WORLD WILL KEEP ON SPINNING
EACH DAY AND EVERY NIGHT

TAKE A LITTLE CHANCE
AND HOLD ON VERY TIGHT
BELIEVE THAT YOU ARE WINNING
WHEN YOUR DREAM IS IN SIGHT

SEAMSTRESS/SON.

WE'RE MOVING IN TIME
OUR WORRIES HAVE GONE

WRITER/ TEACHER.

THE WORDS START TO RHYME
NOW THE RHYTHM IS STRONG

MATCH GIRL/MR SWANN.

WE'RE TURNING AROUND
WE FOLLOW THE SONG

ALL SIX.

A NEW LIFE IS FOUND
AND THE MUSIC PLAYS ON

ALL.

DANCE A LITTLE DANCE
AND STEP INTO THE LIGHT
THE WORLD WILL KEEP ON SPINNING
EACH DAY AND EVERY NIGHT

TAKE A LITTLE CHANCE
AND HOLD ON VERY TIGHT
YOU'VE FOUND A NEW BEGINNING
THE WORLD WILL KEEP ON SPINNING
BELIEVE THAT YOU ARE WINNING
WHEN YOUR DREAM IS IN SIGHT

The Guests dance

*At the end of the dance, everyone exits. Dry ice / smoke
effects start. The music continues into the next scene*

Epilogue   HEAVEN

GOD. Look at them all, dancing and singing down there without a care in the world. All that gold may keep them happy for a while, but it won't secure them a place up here.

The Angel enters carrying a small box containing the lead heart of the Happy Prince

Ah … Angel 4962, do come in. Sit down.

ANGEL. Thank you God. I'm quite exhausted after all that.

GOD. So, this is it. Your day of reckoning. I hope you have been successful in completing the task I set you.

ANGEL. I'll let you be the judge of that.

GOD. Well, I am the judge of everything, so people say. Let's get on with it, empty your pockets and show me what precious things you've found.

ANGEL. Well … it wasn't easy, God. I ended up in a dreary old place with nothing precious anywhere.

GOD. Excuses! Excuses! Angel Gabriel never had this trouble.

ANGEL. I wandered around for ages. Everyone seemed unhappy, until one day, little by little, things started to change.

GOD. Come on now, I haven't got forever. Well, actually I have. But anyway, what have you found?

ANGEL. Well … I began to think that maybe the most precious things in life are often the least obvious.

GOD. Yes … and …

ANGEL. And that they're sometimes found where you least expect them.

GOD. And so …

ANGEL. So I've brought you a dead swallow and the broken lead heart from a statue the people called the Happy Prince.

The Angel gives the box to God

GOD. I see.

God lifts the lid and studies the contents carefully. He closes the lid and smiles kindly

You have chosen well. These two things are indeed precious.

ANGEL. Thank Heavens for that.

GOD. No need, no need. You see, in my garden of paradise this little bird will always sing and in my city of gold the Prince will be truly happy once again. Well done.

ANGEL. (*excitedly*) So do I get my wings?

GOD. Ah yes, your wings. We'll get you measured up right away.

ANGEL. (*turning to leave*) Thank you, Sir.

GOD. (*smiling*) Thank *you*, Angel 4962.

The Angel exits happily

God opens the box, takes out the broken lead heart and looks at it

The heart of the Happy Prince (*He nods approvingly*) … Hmm.

He places the lead heart into his left inside jacket pocket and gives it a little tap.

And the Swallow.

He places the box on the floor and mimes removing the 'dead Swallow' with both hands.

Come on, little one.

He stands up straight and 'releases' him into the Heavens. We hear the sound of birdsong rising to a crescendo. The sound gradually dies away and the lights fade to a blackout. The dry ice / smoke effects stop

10a BOWS

When the Angel takes his bow he can be seen proudly wearing his hard-earned wings

10b (Encore) WHEN YOUR DREAM IS IN SIGHT

COMPANY.
DANCE A LITTLE DANCE
AND STEP INTO THE LIGHT
THE WORLD WILL KEEP ON SPINNING
EACH DAY AND EVERY NIGHT
TAKE A LITTLE CHANCE
AND HOLD ON VERY TIGHT
YOU'VE FOUND A NEW BEGINNING
THE WORLD WILL KEEP ON SPINNING
BELIEVE THAT YOU ARE WINNING
WHEN YOUR DREAM IS IN SIGHT

10c EXIT

FURNITURE & PROPERTY LIST

Further properties may be added at the director's discretion.

On stage:

Plinth/platform for the **Happy Prince** to stand on
Chair or stool – Scenes 2 & 3
Small Bed with a blanket – Scenes 2 & 3
Desk with candle, quill pen, ink bottle and pieces of paper with
writing on them, chair, fire grate with dying embers & empty log
basket with a large sapphire pre-set inside it – Scene 5
'Gold leaf' pre-set in glitter drop – Scene 8

Off stage:

Golf club – a putter (**God**)
Astronomy book (**Thomas**)
Stick with a bundle tied to the end of it (**Swallow**)
Ball gown with passion flower embroidery (**Seamstress**)
Large Ruby (**Seamstress**)
Binoculars (**Teacher**)
Bird book (**Teacher**)
Lantern (**Town Clerk**)
Mobile phone (**Angel**)
Tray of matches with a strap so it can be worn around the neck and
held horizontally. One match box has a large sapphire pre-set inside
it (**Match Girl**)
Penny (**Townsperson**)
Three pennies (**Town Clerk**)
Small model (or puppet) of a dead swallow (**Swallow**)
Ball tickets (**Townspeople**)
White blossom petals (**School Children**)
Ball masks (if required) (**Townspeople**)
Engagement ring (**Cecily**)
A small box containing a lead heart (**Angel**)
Angel's wings for the curtain call (**Angel**)

EFFECTS PLOT

Cue 1   At the end of the **Overture** 21
        Dry ice / smoke effects
Cue 2   **The Angel exits** 22
        Stop the dry ice / smoke effects
Cue 3   **God rings his bell** 22
        A bell effect, eg Triangle
Cue 4   **The Swallow sits at the feet of the Happy Prince** 34
        Single teardrop effect, eg Triangle
Cue 5   **Swallow "…the stars are clear and bright and** 34
        yet it's raining."
        Single teardrop effect, eg Triangle
Cue 6   **The Happy Prince 'comes to life'** 34
        A tinkle of bells, eg Mark Tree
Cue 7   **The Swallow reaches for the ruby** 37
        A tinkle of bells, eg Mark Tree
Cue 8   **The Swallow reaches for a sapphire** 53
        A tinkle of bells, eg Mark Tree
Cue 9   **The Swallow reaches for a sapphire** 59
        A tinkle of bells, eg Mark Tree
Cue 10 **The Swallow reaches for the gold leaf** 62
        A tinkle of bells, eg Mark Tree
Cue 11 **Dreamy Child "It's from the Angel!"** 63
        The 'gold leaf' glitter drop starts – sparingly
        to start with, continuing throughout song 9
        with gradually increasing amounts
Cue 12 **Townspeople "This isn't a dream, what can it** 65
        all mean?"
        The 'gold leaf' glitter drop stops abruptly
Cue 13 **The Happy Prince slowly bows his head and.** 65
        places both hands on his heart
        A tinkle of bells, eg Mark Tree
Cue 14 **At the end of the song 10 as the company exit** 72
        Dry ice / smoke effects
Cue 15 **God releases the Swallow** 74
        *Recorded sound of birdsong rising to a crescendo
        then fading into nothing.
        The dry ice /smoke effects stop

* sound effect available from Samuel French Inc

Other titles by
DAVID PERKINS & CAROLINE DOOLEY,
published by Samuel French Ltd (UK):

The Selfish Giant

Other titles by
DAVID PERKINS
with lyricist **JENIFER TOKSVIG,**
published by Samuel French Ltd (UK):

The Curious Quest
for the Sandman's Sand

Skool & Crossbones

Shake, Ripple & Roll

Pandemonium!
(a Greek Myth-adventure)

For more information,
visit www.dp-music.co.uk

CPSIA information can be obtained at www.ICGtesting.com
Printed in the USA
BVOW06s1422170915

418480BV00008B/26/P